RM. 201

THE HOUSE SITTERS

BY KELLY ROGERS
ILLUSTRATED BY BETSY PETERSCHMIDT

Spellbound

An Imprint of Magic Wagon
abdopublishing.com

*For Bryan, My greatest supporter in this
adventure and those to come. —KRP*

*To Dad: for keeping an eye out for us,
especially for lava. Phew! —BP*

abdopublishing.com

Published by Magic Wagon, a division of ABDO, PO Box
398166, Minneapolis, Minnesota 55439. Copyright © 2017 by
Abdo Consulting Group, Inc. International copyrights reserved
in all countries. No part of this book may be reproduced in
any form without written permission from the publisher.
Spellbound™ is a trademark and logo of Magic Wagon.

Printed in the United States of America, North Mankato,
Minnesota.
052016
092016

 THIS BOOK CONTAINS
RECYCLED MATERIALS

Written by Kelly Rogers
Illustrated by Betsy Peterschmidt
Edited by Heidi M.D. Elston and Megan M. Gunderson
Designed by Candice Keimig

Library of Congress Cataloging-in-Publication Data

Names: Rogers, Kelly, 1981- author. | Peterschmidt, Betsy, illustrator.

Title: The house sitters / by Kelly Rogers ; illustrated by Betsy Peterschmidt.

Description: Minneapolis, MN : Magic Wagon, [2017] | Series: Rm. 201 |
    Summary: Rory and Felix are housesitting for the sinister science teacher
    Ms. Fleek, and she has given them a very specific list of duties, including making
    sure the basement door is locked--but when one day they find the door open and
    venture into the basement, what they find there convinces them that they never
    want to go to that house again.

Identifiers: LCCN 2016002430 (print) | LCCN 2016005837 (ebook) | ISBN
    9781624021688 (lib. bdg.) | ISBN 9781680790474 (ebook)

Subjects: LCSH: Horror tales. | Housesitting--Juvenile fiction. | Secrecy--Juvenile
    fiction. | Science teachers--Juvenile fiction. | CYAC: Horror stories. |
    Housesitting--Fiction. | Secrets--Fiction. | Teachers--Fiction.

Classification: LCC PZ7.1.R65 Ho 2016 (print) | LCC PZ7.1.R65 (ebook) | DDC
    813.6--dc23

LC record available at http://lccn.loc.gov/2016002430

TABLE OF CONTENTS

CHAPTER 1
Help Wanted

FROM: MS. FLEEK
TO: ALL SCIENCE CLASSES
MESSAGE: IN SEARCH OF HOUSE SITTER FOR SPRING BREAK. MUST DO SOME CLEANING. FAIR PAY. NO NONSENSE!

I saw the message on our class website. The first thing I did was **text** Rory. He's my best friend.

Felix

You see Fleek's message?

Rory

Yup. Want to make some cash?

I paused. Ms. Fleek was a bit . . . well, she was a bit **strange**. I didn't know if I wanted to go to her house. But I did want the **CASH**.

Felix

Okay

I made Rory talk to Ms. Fleek. Her classroom smelled like gerbils. And there was a door marked NO STUDENTS EVER. I hated going to RM. 201 for class. I definitely didn't want to go after school.

"We got the job!" Rory told me at the bike rack.

My heart *jumped*. I took a deep breath and told myself I was just **excited** to get the cash. That's all.

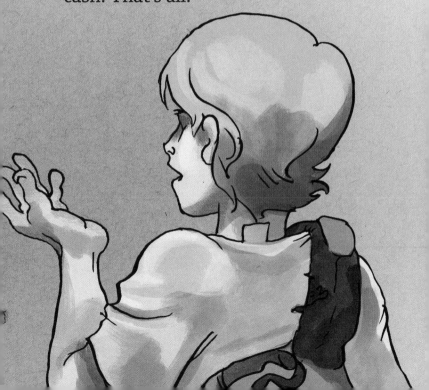

CHAPTER 2

The To-Do List

To Rory and Felix,

Here are the chores that must be completed every day. Do not go upstairs. Do not go downstairs. Do not go into my bedroom. No nonsense!

1. Turn the plants. They cannot get too much sun on one side.

2. Dust the dog figurines.

3. Make sure the dog figurines are facing each other.

4. Dust all surfaces.

5. Water the plants.

6. Make sure the basement door stays locked.

And so, every day I rode my **bike** to meet Rory. Together, we went to Ms. Fleek's house.

We turned the **PLANTS**, so that no one side got too much sun.

We dusted the dog **FIGURINES**.

Rory pretended that one dog was **throwing up** on the others.

"Stop it, man," I told him, laughing. "That's **gross**." Then I made the dogs face each other.

12

"What does *Dust all surfaces*
even mean?" I asked Rory. "Is the
floor a surface? Are the counters?
The kitchen table?"

Rory used the duster on all of
the TABLES. I used spray cleaner on
the kitchen **counter**.

Surfaces:

DONE!

To **WATER** the plants, I found a measuring cup in the kitchen. I **memorized** where to put it back at the end of the week.

I did not like to think about the last thing on the *list*, the basement door.

"Why would the basement door be open?" Rory asked. "If she **locked** it, why do we have to check it every day?"

Of course, I wondered the same thing.

Every day, the last thing
we did was **check** the
basement door. Every day, the
door was *locked*.

CHAPTER 3
Lots of Jars

The **SIXTH** afternoon began like the other five. We turned and watered the plants. We dusted the dogs. We wiped down the surfaces.

But the basement door was unlocked.

It was not just unlocked. It was a
little bit **open**.

"Hey! Felix!" Rory *CALLED*.

I came from the living room. I
had been straightening those strange
dogs. I saw the **basement**
door right away.

I did not like what I *saw*.

"What did you do?" I asked.

"It was like this when I got here!" Rory EXCLAIMED.

"Lock it! I'm done with the dogs. Let's go!" I tried very hard to keep *calm*. Even though my hands were SHAKING.

Rory looked at the **open door**. He looked at me. He looked at the door again.

"Or . . ." said Rory, *slowly*.

"Or . . . ?" I *asked*.

"Or, we could **see** what's down there."

I **DID NOT** like that idea. I did not like that idea **AT ALL**. But before I could talk, Rory was already starting down the stairs. The idea of staying **alone** upstairs was worse. So I followed my friend down into the **basement**.

I could feel it right away. The air was different. **THICK**.

I felt a little dizzy. My throat felt tight. My stomach felt sick. Rory didn't say anything. But I could see that he felt a little sick, too.

The basement was small. It was almost EMPTY.

At the bottom of the stairs, there was one brick wall with shelves. And on those shelves were jars. Lots and lots of jars.

Rory had stopped moving forward. He was BENT OVER at the waist, holding his head in his hands.

But we had come this far. I had to *see* what was in those jars. I kept going.

As I got closer, I saw there was NOTHING in the jars. But each jar had a label.

I scanned my eyes along the
row of jars, reading the LABELS
out loud. "Wouldn't join study
group, 4/1/1987. Dropped an egg,
8/26/1994. Sang songs too loudly,
12/24/1978."

What did these labels mean?
And why had Ms. Fleek labeled
EMPTY jars?

"We should go back," Rory said,
still holding his **head** in his hands.

I turned to go. Then I saw it. A
broken jar.

CHAPTER 4
The Broken Jar

The jar was **smashed** on the floor. I looked closely at the label. It said, "Told rumors in the teachers' lounge, 2/20/1969."

Rory looked at me. I looked at Rory. We turned to **RUN** back up the stairs.

That's when we saw *her*. A woman was standing in the CORNER of the basement. She looked like she was from a different era.

Even though the basement was dark, there was a GLOW around her. She looked very **SCARED**.

"*Where* am I?" the woman asked. "*How* did I get here?"

I stood there with my mouth gaping **OPEN**.

"I was *unlocking* my car, leaving work. Now I'm . . . here.

Wherever here is," she said.

I looked at Rory then back at the woman. I took a big breath and answered. "This is our science teacher's house," I said. "Ms. Fleek."

The woman gasped. Her face **lost** all of its color. "Ms. Fleek? Emily Fleek?"

Rory shrugged. I nodded.

The woman **SOBBED**. But just once. She covered her mouth with her hands. Then she took a breath.

"You two should **LEAVE**!" she said. "You boys, stay as **FAR AWAY** from Emily Fleek as you can." And then she turned and *ran up* the stairs.

Rory and I looked at each other.
We didn't talk. We just started
WORKING. Rory grabbed a broom
and dustpan. I got a plastic bag.

We very carefully cleaned up
the broken jar. We put the
pieces in the bag. We *locked* the
basement door.

We left Ms. Fleek's house.
On the way home, we threw the
bag into a dumpster.

39

We did not go **back** to Ms. Fleek's house.

At school on Monday, Ms. Fleek asked for us. She was coming out of the **NO STUDENTS EVER** door.

I saw the inside for just a second. There were rows of shelves. On them, were dozens of **EMPTY** jars.

Was there something written on one? I couldn't read *FAST* enough. Then she **locked** the door.

"Do you boys have anything to tell me?" asked Ms. Fleek.

It was very hard not to look at Rory. "No," I said. The air felt like that basement air. **THICK**. My stomach felt sick.

I could tell Rory felt it, too.

"No," said Rory.

His face was PALE again.

Ms. Fleek's eyes BURNED into mine.

"I have your **MONEY**,"
Ms. Fleek said. She pushed an
envelope toward us.

Rory looked at me then
pushed away the envelope.
"No, **thank you**,
Ms. Fleek."

"We were happy to
help out," I said.
Ms. Fleek took back the
envelope.

Ms. Fleek looked at us for a long time. "Well," she finally said, "what are you waiting for? Go to class!"

We never talked about that week as Ms. Fleek's HOUSE SITTERS.

We tried to **STAY AWAY** from RM. 201. But we still had to go there for science class.

When I walked by the NO STUDENTS EVER door, the air felt a little **THICK**. I felt a little dizzy. My stomach felt a little sick.

Every time I **LEFT** her room, I wrote a big ✗ over the day in my planner.

One day closer to **NEVER** having to go into RM. 201 again.